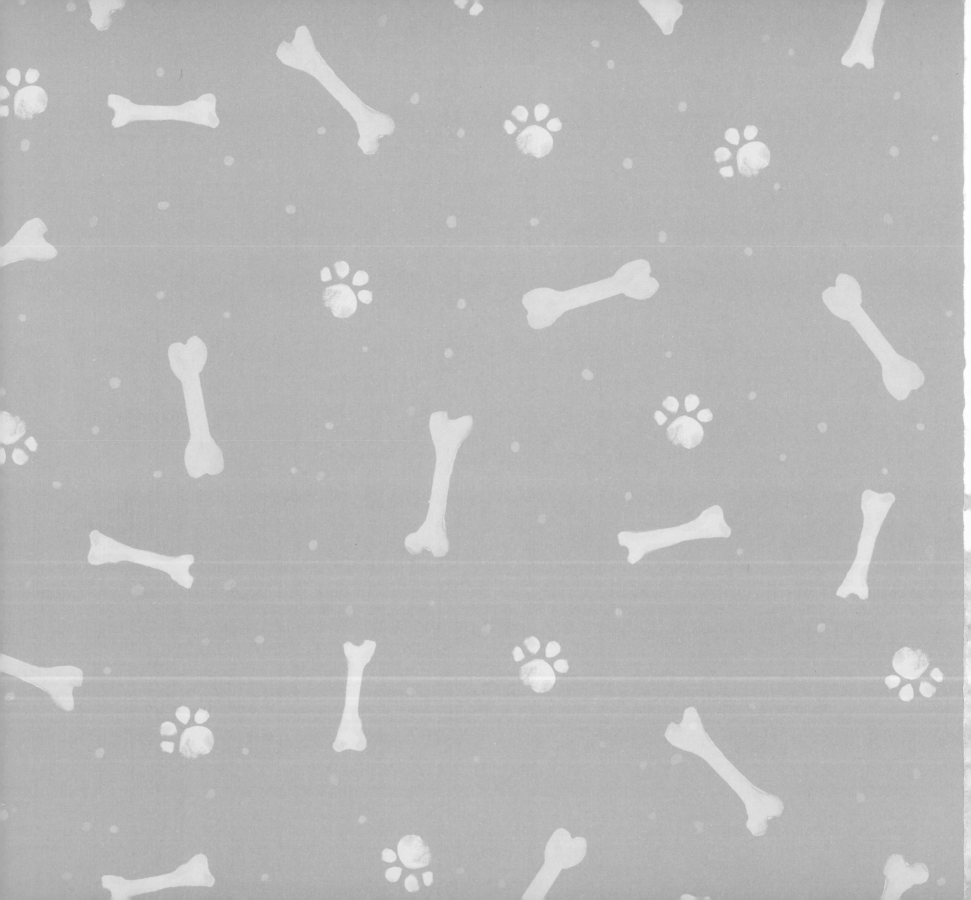

WHERE BONE?

Kitty Moss

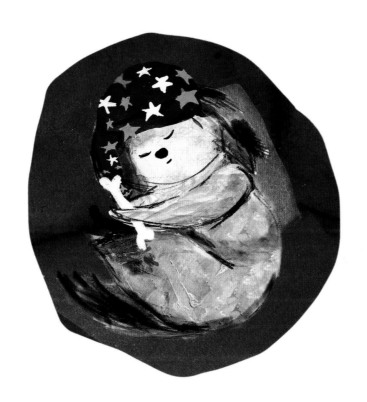

PAGE
STREET
KIDS

GONNA GETCHA BONE

bone in garden?
Balthazar bury Bone?

pond-pond
have bone?
no bone.

big tree
have bone?
no bone.

muck
have bone?
no bone.

Bone? must be home-home

Deep breaths, Balthazar...
stay calm, will find bone

maybe bone with yummies?

must KEEP CALM!
will find Bone

unless...

mischievous mice
have bone?

fishy fisherson
have bone?

pesky parrots
have bone?

clever cat Custard
have bone?

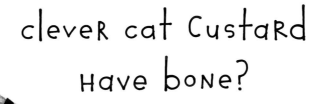

NO BONE!

Keep calm, Balthazar...
bone take swimmies?

no bone

you Bone?

OH
WHERE
BONE?

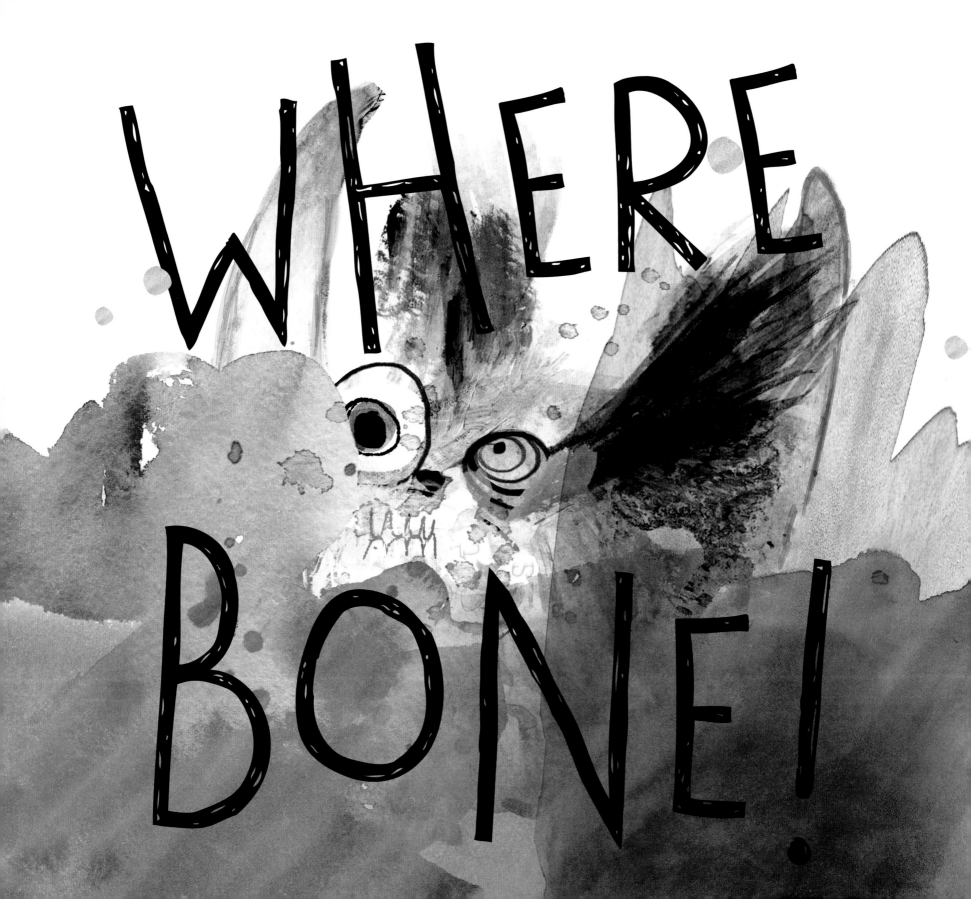

sweet bone, lost forever

look again tomorrow

OH so sleepy...
now Balthazar go bed-bed

Bed!!

BED
MUST
HAVE
BONE!

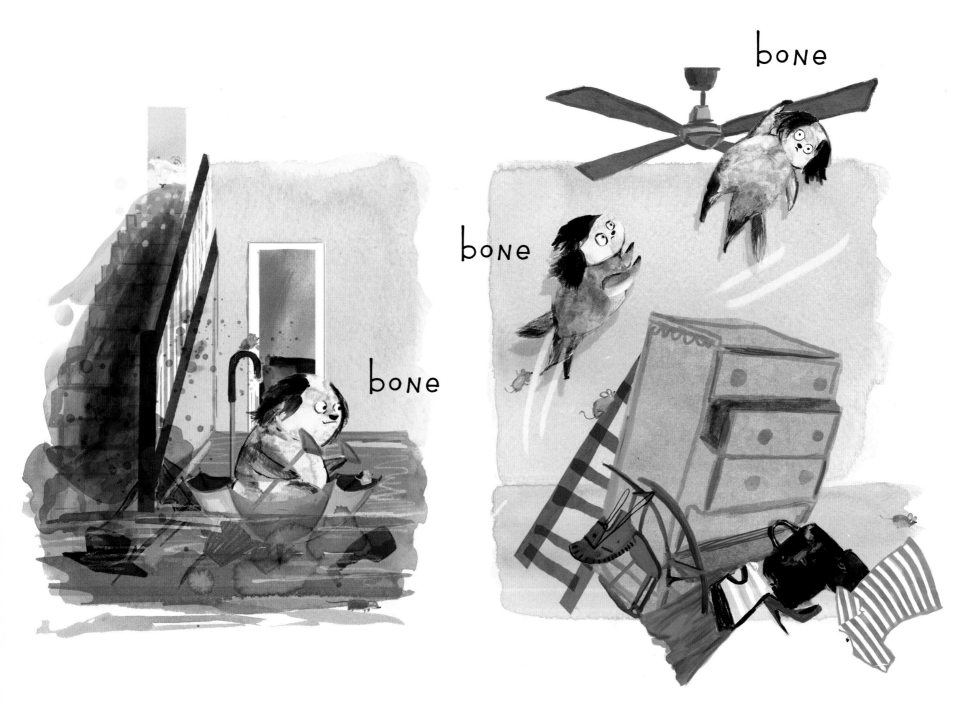

bone

bone

bone

HeRe
bone...?

dear Bone,
it really you!

BEST
FRIEND

knew Bone would be here

For my mum, who actively encouraged my creativity.
For my husband, who provided ample inspiration, support, silliness, and sanity.
For Daisy, who didn't like the sad mice.
For the best boys of my life, Digby Russell, Billy Nini Toes, and Grantie Beavis.
And last but not least, for little Willow Babbins—may the road rise up to meet you.